the Customer at Table 5

Holly Lynden

The Customer At Table 5
Copyright © 2021 by Holly Lynden

Tellwell Talent
www.tellwell.ca

ISBN
978-0-2288-4589-8 (Hardcover)
978-0-2288-4590-4 (Paperback)

To Colby and Cooper. Always be you.

The NoodleNut café was very busy that Saturday afternoon. All the waiter-birds were flitting and fluttering between tables, trying to take orders and deliver food. None of them seemed to notice the customer at table 5, who sat waiting, patiently.

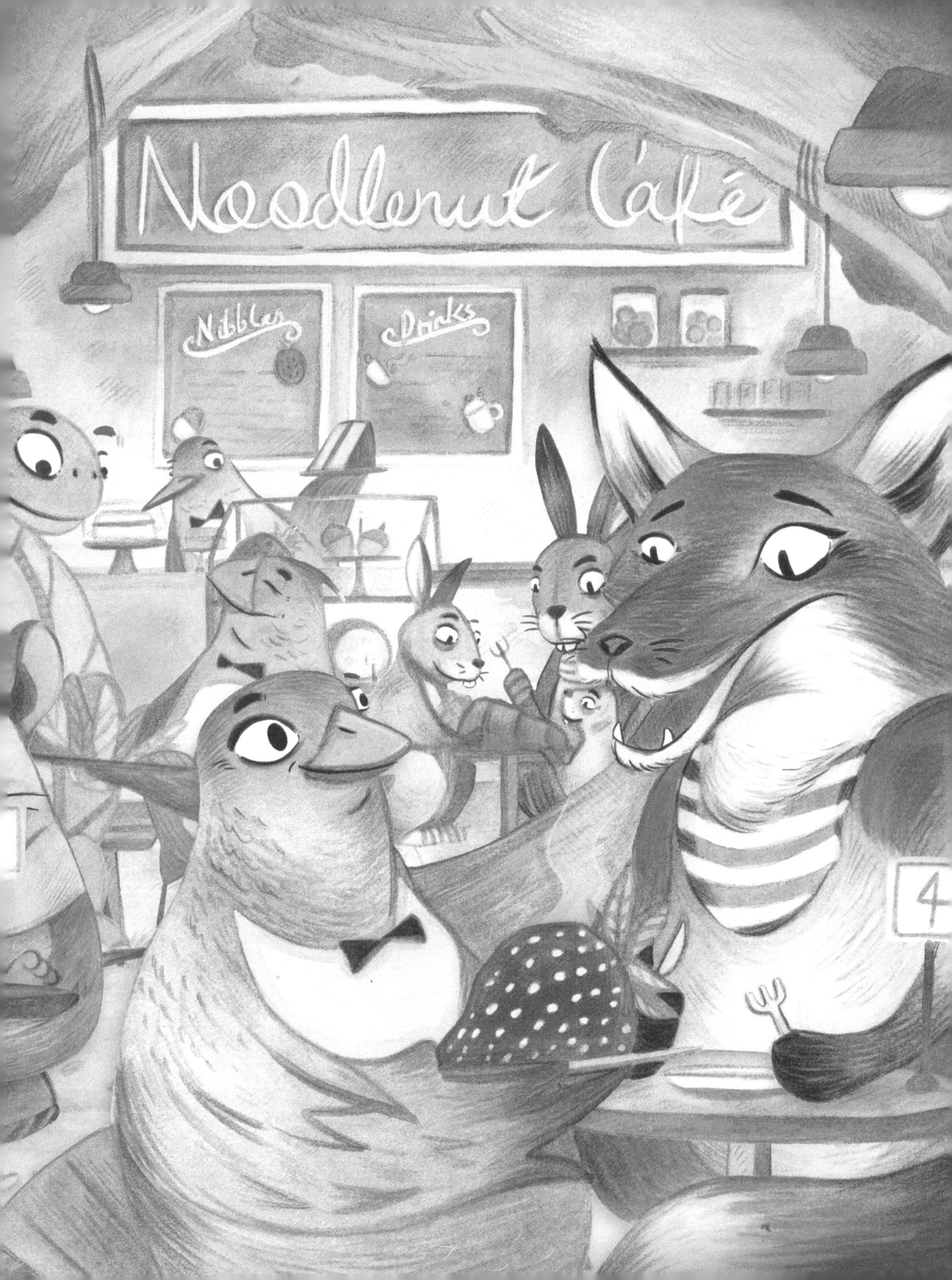
Noodlenut Café
Nibbles
Drinks
4

Finally, a blue waiter-bird approached. With his long wing, he held out a big triangle of cheese.

"Here is your order, sir", said the blue waiter-bird with a bow.

"But I didn't order cheese", said the customer at table 5.

The blue waiter-bird looked confused. "But you are a mouse, and mice eat cheese. This cheese is very stinky and delicious."

The customer at table 5 said, "I am not a mouse. I am a chinchilla."

The blue waiter-bird wasn't convinced. "You have a real mouse-y face, with beady little eyes."

The chinchilla replied, "I like my eyes just fine, and I have the face of a chinchilla."

The blue waiter-bird huffed and flew away from the table. "Larry! Take over table 5, will ya?"

A few minutes later, a green waiter-bird swooped down to table 5, carrying a large orange carrot on his wing.

"Your order has arrived, sir", said the green waiter-bird with a flourish.

"But I didn't order a carrot", said the chinchilla.

The green waiter-bird looked puzzled. "But you are a bunny rabbit, and bunny rabbits eat carrots. This one is especially crunchy."

The chinchilla said, "I am not a bunny rabbit. I am a chinchilla."

The green waiter-bird trilled impatiently, "But you are soft and furry with rather big ears, just like a bunny rabbit."

The chinchilla replied, "I like my ears just fine, and I have the soft fur of a chinchilla."

The green waiter-bird frowned and flapped away from the table. "Melvin, table 5 needs you!"

A few minutes later, a yellow waiter-bird zoomed up to table 5, holding an acorn on his outstretched wing.

"Your order, sir", sang the yellow waiter-bird.

"But I didn't order an acorn", said the chinchilla.

The yellow waiter-bird looked suspicious. "But you are a squirrel, and squirrels eat acorns. This one is particularly nutty."

The chinchilla said, "I am not a squirrel. I am a chinchilla."

"But you have a long bushy tail like a squirrel", chirped the yellow waiter-bird, "Although its bushiness could use some work."

The chinchilla replied, "I like my tail just fine. It is the perfect amount of bushiness."

The yellow waiter-bird muttered something under his breath, tucked the acorn under his arm, and sailed over to a larger, purple waiter-bird. The two twittered to each other. The purple waiter-bird disappeared into the kitchen.

Moments later, he strutted over to the chinchilla at table 5. "Alright. The other waiter-birds tell me you are a chinchilla. So here you are. A nice plate of fresh grass."

"I did not order a plate of grass", replied the chinchilla.

"But you are a chinchilla. And chinchillas eat grass!", squawked the purple waiter-bird.

The chinchilla smiled. "That is true. But I don't feel like eating grass today."

The purple waiter-bird cried out in exasperation, "Then what is it that you want??!!"

The customer at table 5 blinked his chinchilla eyes, waved his chinchilla tail, perked up his chinchilla ears and said calmly, "I would like a hot chocolate, please. Heavy on the marshmallows."

CPSIA information can be obtained
at www.ICGtesting.com
Printed in the USA
LVHW072004260121
677557LV00004B/10